About This Book

Title: *Blake Can Skate*

Step: 4

Word Count: 117

Skills in Focus: silent e

Tricky Words: dreams, sidewalk

Ideas For Using This Book

Before Reading:
- **Comprehension**: Discuss with the readers what they think the book may be about. Have they ever skated? If so, what was it like? Share experiences. Then, prompt students to share predictions based on evidence from the cover and any relevant background knowledge.
- **Phonics**: Preview the title and write the words *Blake* and *Skate* on the board. Ask the students what they notice is the same about the words (they have the long *a* made by silent *e*). Point to the pattern, *a_e*. Explain that this is the vowel-consonant-e pattern. The silent *e* makes the vowel before it have a long sound, saying its own name, /ā/. Repeat with story words *like* and *home* to identify the long *i* (i_e) and long *o* (o_e) pattern.

During Reading:
- Have the readers use their fingers to track the words as they read if needed.
- **Decoding**: If stuck on a word, help students say each sound and blend it together smoothly.
- **Comprehension**: Ask the readers to recall the places Blake skates. Prompt students to use transitional words (first, next, then, last) to name the places in sequence.

After Reading:
Discuss the book. Some ideas for questions:
- What can Blake do in his skates?
- Why do you think Blake cannot skate in the house?
- Why might Blake like to skate so much?
- Make a connection to the character. Think of something you enjoy doing as much as Blake. Why do you like it? How does it make you feel?

Blake Can Skate

Text by Leanna Koch

Educational Content by Kristen Cowen

Illustrated by
Troy David Olin

PICTURE WINDOW BOOKS
a capstone imprint

This is Blake.

Blake can lace up his skates.

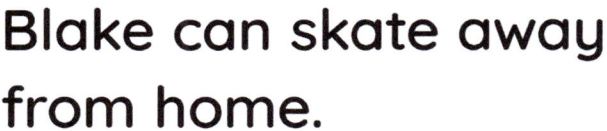

Blake can skate away from home.

Blake can skate past the shops.

Blake can brake. He can stop to get a drink in his skates.

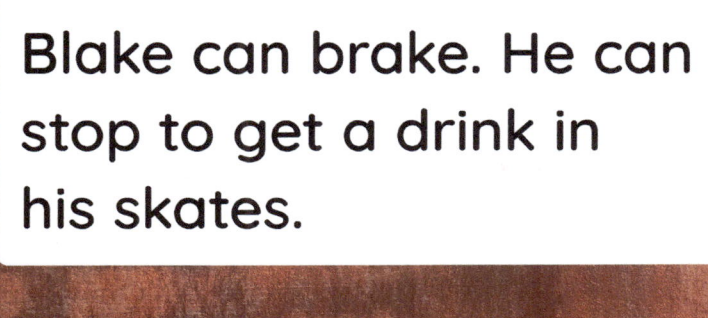

Blake can skate to the lake.

The ducks like Blake's skates.

Blake can skate past the slide.

He can swing in his skates.

Blake can skate home.

Mom tells Blake, "Nope! You can't skate inside."

Blake takes off his skates.

More Activities

Writing with silent e:

In his dreams, Blake can skate anywhere! What do you think he might dream about? Challenge yourself to write a story about Blake's dream using words with the silent *e* pattern. Be creative and have fun!

Suggested silent *e* story words:
Blake, skate, like, slide, inside, home, nope

Extended Learning Activity

Writing- Recall Details

In the story, Blake can skate some places and cannot skate in others. Let's help Blake remember where he is allowed to skate and where he isn't. Using the details from the text, create a list for Blake.

Places Blake **Can** Skate	Places Blake **Cannot** Skate

Published by Picture Window Books,
an imprint of Capstone
1710 Roe Crest Drive,
North Mankato, Minnesota 56003
capstonepub.com

Blake Can Skate was originally published as
Jake Skates, copyright 2007 by Picture Window Books.

Copyright © 2025 by Capstone.
All rights reserved. No part of this publication may be reproduced
in whole or in part, or stored in a retrieval system, or transmitted in
any form or by any means, electronic, mechanical, photocopying,
recording, or otherwise, without written permission of the publisher.

Library of Congress Cataloging-in-Publication Data is available
on the Library of Congress website.

ISBN: 9780756596262 (hardback)
ISBN: 9780756585747 (paperback)
ISBN: 9780756590611 (eBook PDF)